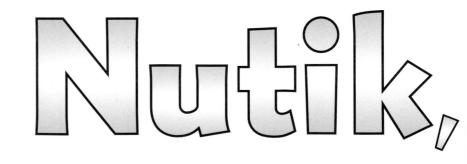

Nutik,

JEAN CRAIGHEAD GEORGE

the Wolf Pup

ILLUSTRATED BY **TED RAND** ⚓ HARPERCOLLINS*PUBLISHERS*

To Chris
–J.C.G.

To Roger Page,
every reader's friend
–T.R.

Nutik, the Wolf Pup Text copyright © 2001 by Julie Productions, Inc. Illustrations copyright © 2001 by Ted Rand Manufactured in China All rights reserved. www.harperchildrens.com
Library of Congress Cataloging-in-Publication Data George, Jean Craighead, date Nutik, the Wolf Pup / Jean Craighead George ; illustrated by Ted Rand p. cm. Summary: When his older sister Julie brings home two small wolf pups, Amaroq takes care of the one called Nutik and grows to love it, even though Julie tells him it cannot stay. ISBN 0-06-028164-2–ISBN 0-06-028165-0 (lib. bdg.) 1. Eskimos–Juvenile Fiction. [1. Eskimos–Fiction. 2. Wolves–Fiction. 3. Brothers and sisters–Fiction. 4. Arctic regions–Fiction.] I. Title. II. Rand, Ted.
PZ7.G2933 Wo 2000 99-010501 [E]–dc21 CIP AC Typography by Matt Adamec   3 4 5 6 7 8 9 10 ❖

In an Eskimo village at the top of the world lived a lively little boy. He was not very old, but he could run as fast as a bird's shadow.

When he ran, his father, Kapugen, the great hunter, caught him and lifted him high over his head.

When he ran, his mother, Ellen, caught him and hugged him closely.

When he ran, his big sister, Julie, caught him and carried him home to tell him wolf stories.

She told him how a wolf pack had saved her life when she was lost and starving on the vast tundra. The wolf pack's noble black leader had shared his family's food with her.

The wolf's name was Amaroq.

The little boy's name was Amaroq.

One day Julie came home with two pups. They were hungry and sickly. She put one in Amaroq's arms.

"Feed and tend this pup," she said. "His name is Nutik. I will feed and tend the other pup. I named her Uqaq. When they are fat and well, the wolves will come and get them."

Amaroq hugged his pup. He felt the little wolf heart beat softly. He kissed the warm head.

"Amaroq," Julie said when she saw this, "do not come to love this wolf pup. I have promised the wolves we will return the pups when they are fat and well."

Amaroq looked into Nutik's golden eyes. The wolf pup licked him and wagged his tail. Julie frowned.

"Don't fall in love, Amaroq," she warned again, "or your heart will break when the wolves come and take him away."

"No, it won't," he said.

Julie gave Amaroq a bottle of milk to feed to his pup. Amaroq wrapped Nutik in soft rabbit skins, and they snuggled down on the grizzly-bear rug.

Every day Amaroq fed Nutik many bottles of milk, bites of raw meat, and bones to chew.

When the moon had changed from a crescent to a circle and back again, Nutik was fat. His legs did not wobble. His fur gleamed. He bounced and woofed. When Amaroq ran, Nutik ran.

Summer came to the top of the world. The sun stayed up all day and all night for three beautiful months.

Because of this, Amaroq and Nutik lived by a different clock.

They fell asleep to the gabble of baby snow geese.

They awoke to the raspy hiss of snowy owlets.

They ate when they were hungry. They slept when they were tired, and they played wolf games in shadow and sun. They were never apart.

"Don't fall in love with Nutik," Julie warned again when the midnight sun was riding low. "I hear the wolves calling. Soon they will come for their pups." She looked at him. "Be strong."

"I am strong," he answered. "I am Amaroq."

One morning Amaroq and Nutik were tumbling on the mossy
tundra when the wolf pack called. They were close by.

"Come home. Come home," they howled.

Nutik heard them.

Uqaq and Julie heard them.

Amaroq heard them. He got to his feet and ran.

Nutik stopped listening to the wolves and ran after him.

Amaroq led Nutik as fast as a falling star. He led him
down a frost heave. He led him around the village
schoolhouse. He led him far from the wolves.

After a long time he led Nutik home. Julie was at the door.

"Uqaq has returned to her family," she said. "The wolves came and got her. Nutik is next."

"I am very tired," Amaroq said, and he rubbed his eyes.

Julie put him to bed in his bearskin sleeping bag. When Julie tiptoed away, Nutik wiggled into the sleeping bag too. He licked Amaroq's cheek.

The sun set in August. The days grew shorter until there was no day at all. Now it was always nighttime.

In the blue grayness of the winter night the wolves came to the edge of the village.

When everyone was sleeping, they called to Nutik.

Nutik crawled out of Amaroq's sleeping bag and gently awakened him. He took his hand in his mouth and led him across the room. He stopped before Amaroq's parka. Amaroq put it on. Nutik picked up a boot. Amaroq put on his boots.

Nutik whimpered at the door.

Amaroq opened it. They stepped into the cold.

The wolves were prancing and dancing like ice
spirits on the hill.

Nutik took Amaroq's mittened hand and led him toward
his wolf family. The frost crackled under their feet. The
wolves whispered their welcome.

Suddenly Amaroq stopped. Nutik was taking him to his wolf home.

"No, Nutik," he said. "I cannot go with you. I cannot live with your family." Nutik tilted his head to one side and whimpered, "Come."

"You must go home alone," Amaroq said, and hugged his beloved wolf pup for a long time.

Then he turned and walked away. He did not run.

Nutik did not chase him.

"I am very strong," Amaroq said to himself.

He got home before his tears froze.

Amaroq crawled into his bearskin sleeping bag and sobbed.
His heart was broken after all.

At last he fell asleep.

Julie awoke him for breakfast.

"I don't want to eat," he told her. "Last night the wolves
came and took Nutik away."

"You are a strong boy," she said. "You let him go back to his
family. That is right."

Amaroq did not eat lunch. When Kapugen took him out
to fish, he did not fish. Tears kept
welling up. He ran home to hide them in
his bearskin sleeping bag.

It was surprisingly warm.

Up from the bottom and into Amaroq's arms wiggled the furry wolf pup.

"Nutik," Amaroq cried joyfully. He hugged his friend and glanced at Julie. Instead of scolding him, she stepped outside.

"Dear wolves," she called across the tundra. "Your beautiful pup, Nutik, will not be coming back to you. He has joined our family.

"Amaroq loves Nutik. Nutik loves Amaroq. They are brothers now. He cannot leave."

As if listening, the wind stopped blowing. In the stillness Julie called out clearly and softly:

"I shall take care of him as lovingly as you took care of me."

And the wolves sang back, "That is good."